Barnyard Buddies

In the Goat Yard

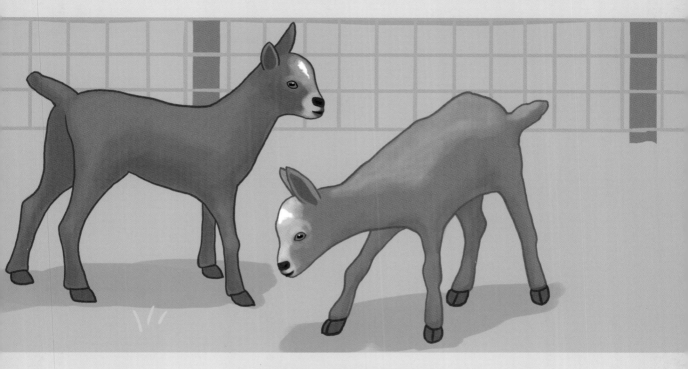

by Patricia M. Stockland
illustrated by Todd Ouren

Special thanks to content consultant:
James S. Cullor, DVM, PhD

magic
Wagon

visit us at www.abdopublishing.com

Published by Magic Wagon, a division of the ABDO Group, 8000 West 78th Street, Edina, Minnesota 55439. Copyright © 2010 by Abdo Consulting Group, Inc. International copyrights reserved in all countries. All rights reserved. No part of this book may be reproduced in any form without written permission from the publisher.

Looking Glass Library™ is a trademark and logo of Magic Wagon.

Printed in the United States.

 Manufactured with paper containing at least 10% post-consumer waste

Text by Patricia M. Stockland
Illustrations by Todd Ouren
Edited by Amy Van Zee
Interior layout and design by Becky Daum
Cover design by Becky Daum

Library of Congress Cataloging-in-Publication Data
Stockland, Patricia M.
  In the goat yard / by Patricia M. Stockland ; illustrated by Todd Ouren.
      p. cm. — (Barnyard buddies)
  Includes index.
  ISBN 978-1-60270-642-2
  1. Goats—Juvenile literature. I. Ouren, Todd, ill. II. Title.
  SF383.35.S76 2010
  636.3'9—dc22
                                      2009007482

The goat pen is shady. The spring morning is cool. A doe calls to her kids. **Baa, baa.**

Baby goats are called kids.

The kids were just born. But soon they stand. They call back to their mother. The kids are hungry.

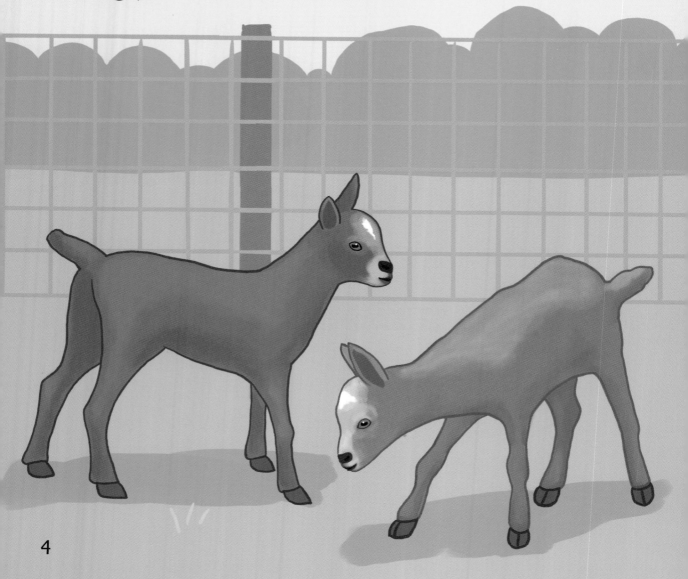

Kids can stand and walk within hours of being born.

The hungry kids drink milk from the doe. Within a few weeks, the kids will begin to eat grasses.

Kids drink milk until they are two or three months old.

The doe takes her kids into the yard. The goat herd is grazing there.

Goats are often kept in fenced yards. The fences help protect the herd from predators.

As the months grow warmer, the kids grow bigger. They learn to eat grasses and grains with the other goats.

Goats eat grasses, hay, corn, oats, and other grains.
Goats also need salt in their diets.

When the kids are a few months old, the farmer weans them from the doe. They are big enough to be on their own.

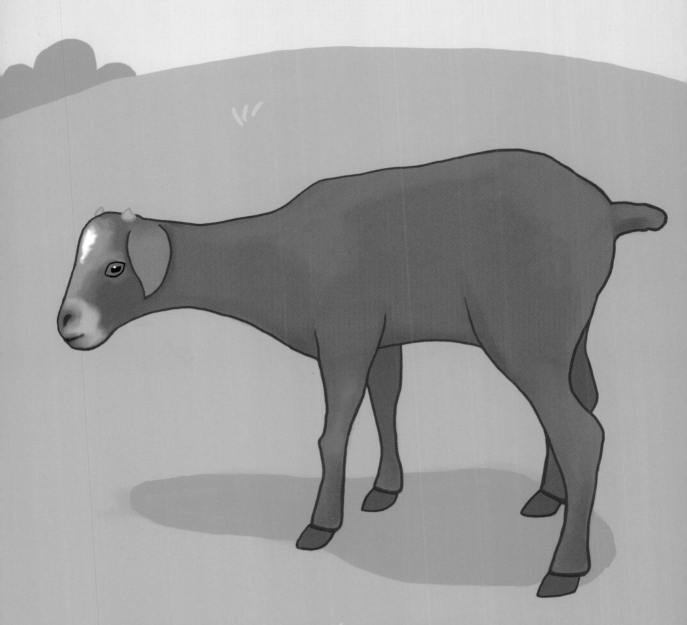

Separating a doe and her kids is called "weaning."

The doe can still give milk. The farmer milks all the does every morning and evening.

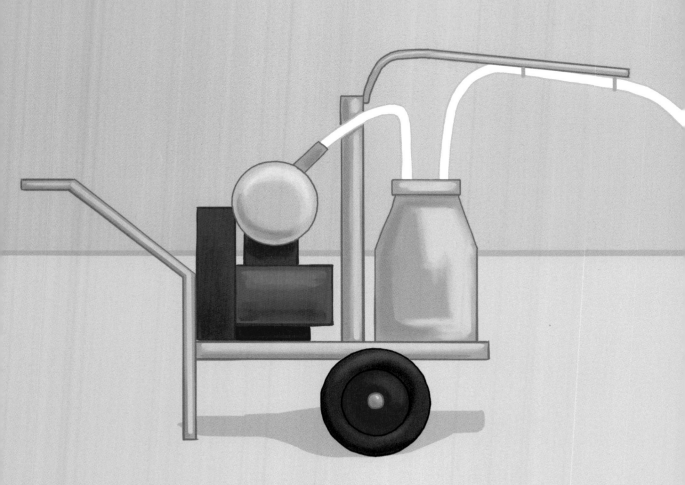

Farmers raise goats for milk, meat, and hides.

Some goats stay on the farm. The farmer takes other goats to market.

Most goats live 8 to 12 years.

The weaned kids play together in the yard.
They jump and run. They nibble new foods.

Goats are very smart and curious.

The kids have grown big and strong. Next spring, the goats will have kids of their own.

Baa, baa, baa!

Goat Diagram

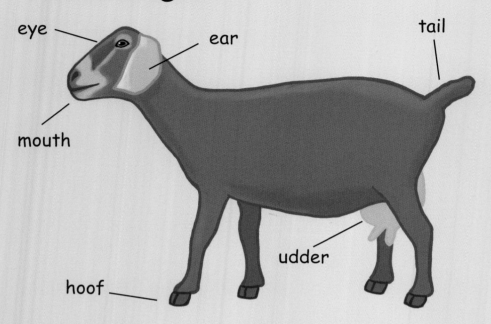

eye

ear

tail

mouth

hoof

udder

Glossary

doe—an adult female goat.

graze—to feed on land covered by grass.

hide—the skin of an animal.

market—where animals are bought and sold.

predator—an animal that hunts other animals.

Fun Facts

 Around the world, more people drink goat milk than cow milk.

 Milk production is measured in pounds. Dairy goats can produce six to eight pounds (3 to 4 kg) of milk per day.

 Some people who are allergic to cow milk can safely drink goat milk.

 A goat's stomach is divided into four parts. These parts help the goat digest its food.

 Goats usually have horns, which are often removed when the kids are very young.

 One breed of goats is called fainting goats. When these goats are frightened or surprised, their muscles stiffen and they tip over. The goats look like they are fainting!

 An adult male goat is called a buck.

 Sometimes, male goats are called billy goats and female goats are called nanny goats.

 Some types of cheese, such as blue cheese and feta cheese, are made from goat's milk.

Index

24